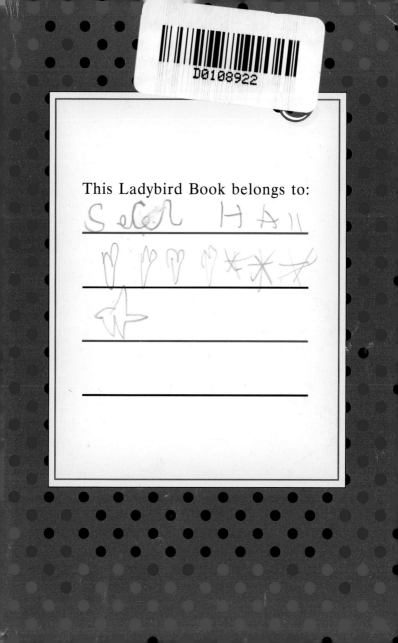

This Ladybird Book belongs to:

Sear Hall

All children have a great ambition … to read by themselves.

Through traditional and popular stories, each title in the **Read It Yourself** series introduces children to the most commonly used words in the English language (*Key Words*), plus additional words necessary to tell the story.
The additional words appearing in this book are listed below.

wife, witch's, garden, lettuce, started, ill, climb, waiting, Rapunzel, tower, hair, prince, hears, singing, doesn't, marry, silk, ladder, hurt, angry, cuts, far, leaves, eyes, cry, tears, talked, kept, wanted, took, married, heard, waited

Ladybird books are widely available, but in case of difficulty may be ordered by post or telephone from:

Ladybird Books – Cash Sales Department
Littlegate Road Paignton Devon TQ3 3BE
Telephone 0803 554761

A catalogue record for this book is available from the British Library

Published by Ladybird Books Ltd Loughborough Leicestershire UK
Ladybird Books Inc Auburn Maine 04210 USA

Ladybird

Rapunzel

adapted by Fran Hunia
from the traditional tale
illustrated by Kathie Layfield

A man and his wife
looked into a witch's garden.

They saw some lettuce.

"That lettuce looks good,"
said the woman.

"Yes," said the man.
"I will get some for you."

"No," said his wife.
"It is the witch's lettuce.
We can't have it."

She kept on looking
at the lettuce. She wanted some
so much.

Soon the woman started
to get ill. "I will have
to get some lettuce
for you," said the man.

He climbed into the witch's
garden and took some lettuce.

He took it home
and gave it to his wife.

She was very pleased
with the lettuce.

The man climbed
into the witch's garden
again.

This time the witch was waiting
and she saw the man get
some lettuce.

"That's my lettuce,"
she said. "Give it to me."

"Please let me have it,"
said the man.
"I want it for my wife.
She is ill."

The witch said, "You can have
the lettuce, but when your wife
has a baby, you must give it
to me."

One day the woman
had a baby girl
and named her Rapunzel.

The witch came to get her.
"Come with me, Rapunzel,
I will give you a good home."

The man and his wife
had to give Rapunzel
to the witch.

They were very sad.

The witch took
Rapunzel away.

She kept her in a tower.

Rapunzel could not get down,
and she had no one
to talk to.

She was very sad.

When the witch
wanted to see Rapunzel,
she went to the tower
and said,
"Rapunzel, Rapunzel,
let your hair down."

Rapunzel let her hair down
to the witch.

She climbed up
Rapunzel's hair
and went into the tower.

One day a prince
came to the tower.

He heard Rapunzel singing.

He looked everywhere for her,
but he could not see her
and he could not get
into the tower.

He went home.
But he wanted to see
Rapunzel, so he came
to the tower again.

The witch came to the tower.
She didn't see the prince.
He heard her say,
"Rapunzel, Rapunzel,
let your hair down."

The prince saw how Rapunzel
let her hair down.

Then he saw the witch
climb up it
and get into the tower.

The prince waited for the witch
to climb down and go home.
Then he went to the tower
and said, "Rapunzel, Rapunzel,
let your hair down."
Then he climbed up it.

Rapunzel was very pleased
to see him.

They talked and talked.

When the prince
was going home he said,
"Can I come and see you
again, Rapunzel?"

"Yes," said Rapunzel.

The prince kept on coming
to see Rapunzel.

One day he said,
"Please marry me, Rapunzel."

"I want to marry you,"
said Rapunzel.
"But we can't get married
up here in this tower.
I will have to get down.
Can you help me?"

The prince said
that he would help.

"Please get me some silk,"
said Rapunzel.
"I will make a ladder
so that I can climb down."

The prince got some silk
for Rapunzel.

He took it to the tower
and said,
"Rapunzel, Rapunzel,
let your hair down."

Rapunzel let her hair down.

The prince climbed up it
and gave her the silk.

Rapunzel started to make
the ladder.

One day the witch
came to see Rapunzel.

She hurt Rapunzel's hair
when she climbed up it.

Rapunzel said,
"The prince didn't hurt me
when he climbed up my hair."

The witch was very angry.
She cut Rapunzel's hair
and took her away.

Then the witch
waited in the tower
for the prince to come.

The prince came
to the tower
to see Rapunzel.

He said,
"Rapunzel, Rapunzel,
let your hair down."

The witch had
Rapunzel's hair
and she let it down
to the prince.

The prince climbed up
Rapunzel's hair.

He looked for Rapunzel
but he could not see her.

He saw the witch
and he jumped down quickly.

When the prince jumped down,
he hurt his eyes.

Now he could not see.
He walked away sadly.

The prince walked on and on.

One day he heard
a girl singing.

It was Rapunzel.

The prince walked up to her.

Rapunzel was so pleased
to see the prince
that she started to cry.

Her tears went
into the prince's eyes.

The prince could see again.

Rapunzel went home
with the prince
and soon they were married.

LADYBIRD READING SCHEMES

Read It Yourself links with all Ladybird reading schemes and can be used with any other method of learning to read.

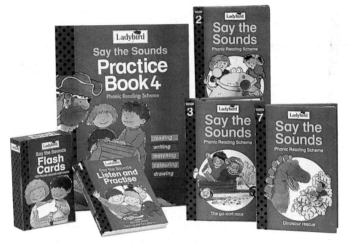

Say the Sounds

Ladybird's **Say the Sounds** graded reading scheme is a *phonics* scheme. It teaches children the sounds of individual letters and letter combinations, enabling them to tackle new words by building them up as a blend of smaller units.

There are 8 titles in this scheme:

1 **Rocket to the jungle**
2 **Frog and the lollipops**
3 **The go-cart race**
4 **Pirate's treasure**
5 **Humpty Dumpty and the robots**
6 **Flying saucer**
7 **Dinosaur rescue**
8 **The accident**

Support material available: Practice Books, Double Cassette pack, Flash Cards

Every new generation of children is enthralled by the famous stories in our Well Loved Tales series. Younger ones love to have the story read to them. Older children will enjoy the exciting stories in an easy-to-read text.

British Library Cataloguing in Publication Data

Southgate, Vera
  The elves and the shoemaker.
  I. Title   II. Stevenson, Peter, *1953-*   III. Grimm, Jacob,
  1785-1863. Elfe und der Schumacher   IV. Series
  823′.914[J]
  ISBN 0-7214-1199-1

Revised edition

Published by Ladybird Books Ltd Loughborough Leicestershire UK
Ladybird Books Inc Auburn Maine 04210 USA

© LADYBIRD BOOKS LTD MCMLXXXIX

Printed in England